PEOPLE AT THE CENTER OF

THE PERSIAN GULF WAR

By DONNA SCHAFFER

**BLACKBIRCH™
PRESS**

THOMSON

GALE

San Diego • Detroit • New York • San Francisco • Cleveland
New Haven, Conn. • Waterville, Maine • London • Munich

THOMSON

GALE

For more information, contact
The Gale Group, Inc.
27500 Drake Rd.
Farmington Hills, MI 48331-3535
Or you can visit our Internet site at http://www.gale.com

Photo credits: cover © Corel Corporation; cover, page 4 © AP Wide World; page 5 © Francoise de Mulder/CORBIS; page 6 © Larry Lee Photography/CORBIS; pages 7, 9, 16, 20, 27, 45 © Jacques Langevin/CORBIS; page 8 © Patrick Durand/ CORBIS SYGMA; page 10-11, 22, 26, 30, 41 © Peter Turnley/CORBIS; cover, pages 12, 25, 37, 39 © Hulton/Archive; page 13 © Reuters/New Media Inc./CORBIS; pages 14-15, 38 © David Turnley/CORBIS; cover, pages 17, 18-19, 40 © CORBIS; pages 21, 29, 31, 43 © Bettmann/CORBIS; page 31 © Neema Frederic/CORBIS SYGMA; page 33 © Wally McNamee/CORBIS; page 34, 44 © AFP/CORBIS; page 35 © David Rubinger/ CORBIS; page 36 © CORBIS SYGMA; page 42 © Aubert-Milner/ CORBIS SYGMA

LIBRARY OF CONGRESS CATALOGING-IN-PUBLICATION DATA

Schaffer, Donna.
   The Persian Gulf War / by Donna Schaffer and Alfred Meyer.
      p. cm. — (People at the center of:)
   Summary: Profiles people involved in the Persian Gulf War as political or military leaders, including Saddam Hussein, Colin Powell, Margaret Thatcher, and Yitzhak Shamir. Includes bibliographical references and index.
   ISBN 1-56711-767-8
   1. Persian Gulf War, 1991—Juvenile literature. [1. Persian Gulf War, 1991.] I. Meyer, Alfred, 1935- II. Title. III. Series.

   DS79.723.S33 2003
   956.7044'2—dc21   2003011062

CONTENTS

THE PERSIAN GULF WAR

Saddam Hussein (above) became president of Iraq in 1979. In 1980, he started a war with Iran (oposite) that lasted eight years.

The name *Saddam in* Arabic means "one who confronts." The president of Iraq, Saddam Hussein, has at least twice lived up to that meaning. He did so when he started a war with Iran in 1980, and then again when he invaded Kuwait in 1990.

A border dispute sparked the war with Iran. It mainly involved the control of a river that runs between the two countries. Large oil fields lie on Iran's side of the river. Saddam believed his army could capture them. It could not, and the war ended in a draw after eight hard-fought years.

The invasion of 1990 also had oil as its goal. Kuwait, a small country on Iraq's southeastern border, was wealthy with oil reserves. Saddam hoped to conquer Kuwait and make it part of Iraq.

On July 17, in a speech made in Baghdad, Iraq's capital, Saddam blamed Kuwait for producing too much oil. He claimed that this action caused world oil prices to drop. As a result, Iraq's earnings from its own oil sales dropped, too. He also accused Kuwait's government of secretly drawing more than its fair share of oil from the Rumaila oil field. This vast field runs beneath both sides of the Iraq-Kuwait border.

Finally, Saddam expressed anger when the leaders of Kuwait refused to forgive the large loans it had made to Iraq during its war with Iran. If he took over Kuwait, his government would not need to repay those loans.

When Iraq invaded Kuwait in 1990, Saddam Hussein claimed that Kuwait produced too much oil and depressed prices.

Many world leaders tried to persuade Saddam to give up his announced plan to invade Kuwait, but their arguments failed. Saddam chose confrontation instead. On August 2, 1990, Iraqi soldiers and tanks crunched into Kuwait. Weakly defended, the country was quickly overrun. Its leader, the emir of Kuwait, escaped to nearby Saudi Arabia within hours. As soon as Saddam's soldiers crossed the border, they began to terrorize Kuwaiti citizens and loot their property.

The international community quickly condemned Iraq's action. Before the day ended, the United Nations demanded that Saddam withdraw his troops at once. Defiant, the Iraqi president instead announced his intention to annex Kuwait and make it part of his country. A large number of Iraqi forces then moved closer to the border between Kuwait and Saudi Arabia. It seemed as if they might attack Saudi Arabia next. It, too, had huge quantities of oil.

Aware of the threat to his country, Saudi Arabia's king asked the United States for military help to prevent any attack. He also invited American forces to take up positions in his country. They began to arrive in the kingdom a day later. Their presence on Saudi soil marked the first stages of Operation Desert Shield. Designed to defend Saudi Arabia, the operation came to include forces from an international coalition formed by the United States and endorsed by the United Nations. Some thirty-five countries eventually joined the coalition.

After Iraq's invasion of Kuwait, soldiers from thirty-five countries, including these from France, formed a coalition to prevent an attack on Saudi Arabia.

In January 1991, hundreds of bombs were dropped on Baghdad as Operation Desert Storm began.

Iraq's leaders took note of the growing force set to keep Iraq from advancing any farther. They chose not to try to invade Saudi Arabia, but they did not withdraw from Kuwait either. Instead, on August 28, Saddam declared the annexation of Kuwait and labeled it the nineteenth province of Iraq. The United Nations responded swiftly. It declared the annexation to be "null and void."

Months passed as both Iraq and the coalition exchanged threats and strengthened their military forces. Diplomatic efforts to prevent armed conflict failed, as they had failed to prevent the invasion of Kuwait in the first place. Nor did the economic sanctions placed on Iraq by the United Nations soften Saddam's hard stance. Sanctions are a way to punish or weaken a country that breaks international law. In this case,

UN member states agreed not to trade with Iraq. This hurt Iraq's economy. The country could not sell its oil to buy such things as food, cars, or weapons.

Saddam's continued refusal to withdraw his troops then prompted coalition military leaders to develop and refine an overall plan. It called for Operation Desert Shield to change into Operation Desert Storm. The coalition now planned to expel Iraqi forces from Kuwait altogether.

In league with the United Nations, at the end of November the coalition gave Iraq a stern deadline. It must leave Kuwait by January 15, 1991, or face military action. Saddam ignored the deadline. Two days later, the coalition unleashed Operation Desert Storm. It started with a thunderous air campaign. Bombs and missiles rained down on Iraqi troop positions, tanks, mobile missile launchers, and radar sites. Saddam responded by launching Scud missiles at Saudi Arabia and Israel. These Soviet-built ballistic missiles can carry chemical, biological, and nuclear warheads.

The ground-war phase of Desert Storm started on February 24, 1991, the day coalition troops attacked Iraqi positions in and around Kuwait. The battle ended in a decisive victory for the coalition just four days later. Its ground forces had overwhelmed the Iraqi army, driven it from Kuwait, and chased it into Iraq. The fighting ended after the coalition declared a cease-fire. The Persian Gulf War came to an official close on April 11 when Iraq formally agreed to UN peace terms.

After only four days of ground fighting, Iraqi soldiers in Kuwait surrendered and Iraq agreed to UN peace terms.

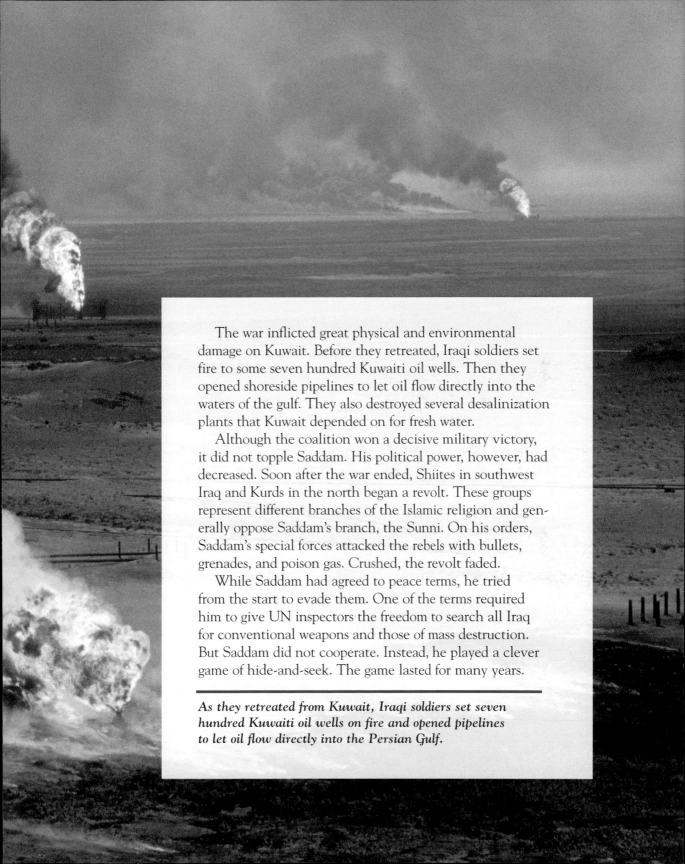

The war inflicted great physical and environmental damage on Kuwait. Before they retreated, Iraqi soldiers set fire to some seven hundred Kuwaiti oil wells. Then they opened shoreside pipelines to let oil flow directly into the waters of the gulf. They also destroyed several desalinization plants that Kuwait depended on for fresh water.

Although the coalition won a decisive military victory, it did not topple Saddam. His political power, however, had decreased. Soon after the war ended, Shiites in southwest Iraq and Kurds in the north began a revolt. These groups represent different branches of the Islamic religion and generally oppose Saddam's branch, the Sunni. On his orders, Saddam's special forces attacked the rebels with bullets, grenades, and poison gas. Crushed, the revolt faded.

While Saddam had agreed to peace terms, he tried from the start to evade them. One of the terms required him to give UN inspectors the freedom to search all Iraq for conventional weapons and those of mass destruction. But Saddam did not cooperate. Instead, he played a clever game of hide-and-seek. The game lasted for many years.

As they retreated from Kuwait, Iraqi soldiers set seven hundred Kuwaiti oil wells on fire and opened pipelines to let oil flow directly into the Persian Gulf.

Born to a poor family in a small northern Iraqi village on April 28, 1937, Saddam Hussein learned to read and write only after he moved to Baghdad at age ten. Encouraged by his uncle, an army officer, he became active in politics. At nineteen, he joined the Ba'ath Party, which at the time was weak in influence. After taking part in a failed attempt to assassinate Iraq's prime minister, Saddam fled to Syria and then Egypt, where he studied law.

Jailed within a year of his return to Baghdad, he escaped and soon became an important figure in the Ba'ath Party. It gained political control of Iraq in 1968. Saddam held several top party posts over the next ten years. He also became an army general and formed a secret police force to fight off any challenges to Ba'ath rule. He became president of Iraq in 1979.

In July 1990, Saddam started to complain publicly about his southern neighbor, Kuwait. He peppered his complaints with grave threats. If his mostly oil-related disputes with Kuwait could not be settled in Iraq's favor, it might then take military action. The Iraqi army at the time ranked as the fourth largest in the world. It had also gained considerable combat experience during the long Iran-Iraq War. Saddam's threats, as a result, alarmed Kuwait, a large number of Arab nations, and the international community.

Instead of responding agreeably to pleas from many world leaders for Iraq to find a peaceful way to settle its disputes, Saddam only intensified his threats. He even promised to blow up most of the oil wells in the Middle East if he did not get his way. To bolster his stance, he massed his troops on Kuwait's border. When the dispute went unresolved, he ordered them to invade. His decision ignited the Persian Gulf War.

The Ba'ath Party took political control of Iraq in 1968. Saddam Hussein (above right and opposite page) held top party posts until becoming Iraqi president in 1979.

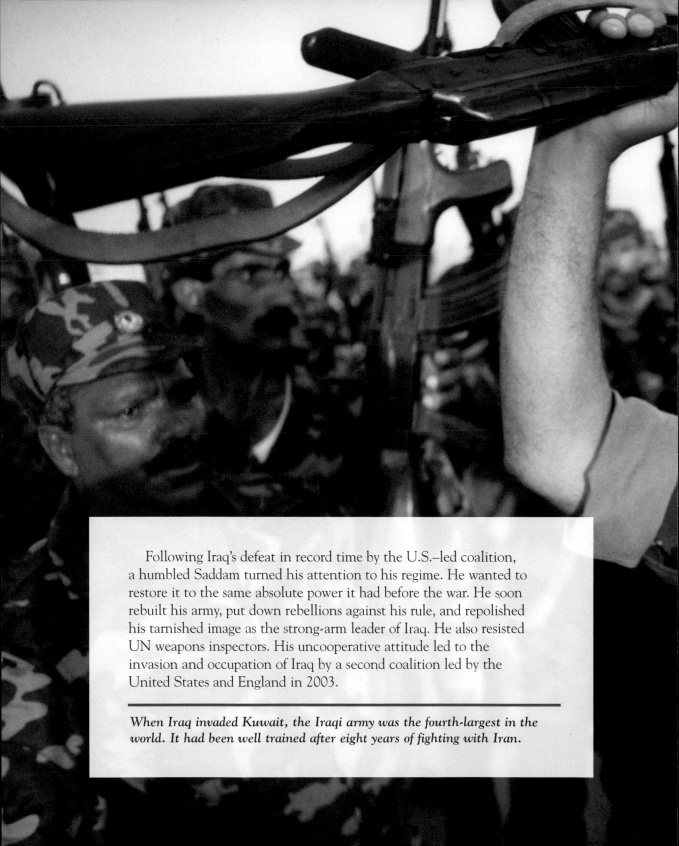

Following Iraq's defeat in record time by the U.S.–led coalition, a humbled Saddam turned his attention to his regime. He wanted to restore it to the same absolute power it had before the war. He soon rebuilt his army, put down rebellions against his rule, and repolished his tarnished image as the strong-arm leader of Iraq. He also resisted UN weapons inspectors. His uncooperative attitude led to the invasion and occupation of Iraq by a second coalition led by the United States and England in 2003.

When Iraq invaded Kuwait, the Iraqi army was the fourth-largest in the world. It had been well trained after eight years of fighting with Iran.

GEORGE H. W. BUSH

Born to a wealthy family on July 24, 1924, George H. W. Bush went on to graduate from Yale College in New Haven, Connecticut, and then moved to Texas to work in the oil industry. He later won a seat in Congress for one term. Afterward, President Richard M. Nixon named him representative to the United Nations. More government appointments followed, which included one as director of the Central Intelligence Agency. After he served eight years as vice president under Ronald Reagan, Bush became president in 1988.

Iraq's attack on Kuwait presented Bush with a serious crisis. He suspected that Saddam Hussein's plans went beyond Kuwait. It was no secret that the Iraqi president wanted to become the strongest Arab ruler in the Middle East. He could do so by next invading Saudi Arabia and maybe also the United Arab Emirates, another oil-rich nation nearby. Bush worried that if Saddam succeeded, he would control a large portion of the world's oil supply. Industrial nations, which depended on oil, might then be at the mercy of Saddam's whims.

When Saddam moved his troops close to the Saudi border, Bush did not hesitate. Iraqi aggression "will not stand," he announced on August 5, 1990. Two days later, he ordered U.S. troops, planes, and warships to the Saudi kingdom to help defend it. He also set in motion diplomatic moves to create an international coalition to resist

In August 1990, President George H. W. Bush (opposite) began preparations for Operation Desert Shield by sending U.S. troops into Saudi Arabia.

Saddam. Partly as a result of these moves, the United Nations condemned the invasion. The world body also slapped Iraq with tough economic sanctions.

Over the next five months, Bush waited to see if armed conflict could be avoided by diplomacy. Not hopeful, he sent a steady stream of American forces to the region. Then, in early January 1991, the president ordered the U.S.–led coalition to eject the Iraqis from Kuwait if they did not withdraw on their own. They did not, and they suffered the consequences.

After the war, Bush received high praise for the effective way in which he had conducted it as the coalition's commander in chief. His popularity in the United States soared. Then, as the presidential election of November 1993 approached, the U.S. economy took a tumble. Unemployment rose, and the stock market fell. The president lost his bid for reelection. Succeeded by Bill Clinton, Bush retired to his home in Houston, Texas.

By January 1991, Iraq still refused to withdraw from Kuwait. President Bush launched Operation Desert Storm, using U.S. troops, planes, and warships to eject Iraqi forces from Kuwait.

The first woman to serve as prime minister of England, Margaret Thatcher held that office from 1979 to 1990. Born on October 13, 1925, she had studied chemistry at Oxford before studying law and entering politics. Because of her strong political views, she later became known as the "Iron Lady."

Thatcher believed that England's government was too large and costly, so she worked to reduce it. Since American president Ronald Reagan held similar views about the U.S. government, the two leaders struck up a close personal friendship. Thatcher's relationship with President George H. W. Bush was less close but cordial.

After Iraq invaded Kuwait, British Prime Minister Margaret Thatcher (opposite) pledged England's support, including tanks (above).

By coincidence, Thatcher had just arrived in Aspen, Colorado, the day Iraq invaded Kuwait. She had come to speak at the same conference that Bush would also address. The two leaders met the morning before the conference began.

The president asked Thatcher for her view of the invasion. She did not hesitate to condemn it, and added that dictators like Saddam must be stopped. She also warned that if he went on to gain major control of the world's oil resources, he could then wage economic war against industrialized nations.

Although the president listened to differing opinions from some of his advisers, he soon agreed with the prime minister. Firmly convinced she was right, he decided to openly oppose Iraq. Before she returned home, Thatcher also assured the president that England could be counted on to participate in any military showdown with Saddam Hussein. British troops, planes, and ships soon joined U. S. forces in the Persian Gulf.

Soon afterward, Thatcher lost a crucial Conservative Party election. She resigned as prime minister and was replaced by John Major in November 1990, six weeks before Operation Desert Storm unfolded. Following her lead, Major reconfirmed England's pledge to provide significant support to the coalition.

After Thatcher left office, she became Lady Margaret Thatcher when Queen Elizabeth awarded her the title "Dame of the British Empire," a title of great distinction in England. Thatcher went on to hold a seat in the House of Lords, the upper house in Parliament, where her title became Baroness Thatcher of Kesteven.

MIKHAIL GORBACHEV

Born March 2, 1931, on a large Soviet farm, Mikhail Gorbachev first joined the Communist Party while a law student at Moscow University. He rose steadily in party ranks and became an expert in the Soviet Union's agricultural affairs. He succeeded Leonid Brezhnev as secretary–general of the Soviet Union in 1985. His goal was to make his country's government more modern, efficient, and democratic. He also wanted to improve relations with the West. In 1987, he and U.S. president Ronald Reagan reached a historic agreement to end the highly expensive arms race between the two countries. Tensions eased around the world when the Cold War ended. It was called "Cold" because its two main rivals, the Soviet Union and the United States, never started a real or "hot" war between them.

Even though the Soviet Union teetered on the brink of economic collapse in 1990, Gorbachev had by then won international acclaim for having helped end the Cold War. Many people saw him as a peacemaker of great influence. Shortly after Saddam Hussein began to threaten Kuwait, Gorbachev approached him. The Soviet leader suggested that Saddam pursue a peaceful path in its relations with Kuwait. Saddam rejected the idea. Like so many others, Gorbachev could not coax the Iraqi president to change course.

Afterward, Gorbachev decided to back the United States and the United Nations. Two days after the invasion of Kuwait, the Soviet Union and the United States issued a joint statement that condemned the invasion. This came as a blow to Saddam, who expected the same approval and military aid the Soviets had provided him in the past. Instead, he now found the world's two superpowers allied against him. While the Soviet Union did not provide combat troops to the coalition's war effort, Gorbachev's decision prompted other Communist countries to join the campaign against Iraq.

In his own country, Gorbachev's hold on power had dramatically slipped. He resigned in December 1991 after the Soviet Union broke up and was replaced by a loose alliance of former Soviet republics, chief among them Russia. Gorbachev attempted a political comeback in 1996 when he sought election as Russia's president. He drew less than 2 percent of the vote. He then devoted himself to writing books.

When Saddam began to threaten Kuwait, Mikhail Gorbachev tried unsuccessfully to convince him to not to invade Kuwait.

FRANÇOIS MITTERRAND

TRIED TO PERSUADE SADDAM TO WITHDRAW FROM KUWAIT

François Mitterrand was born on October 26, 1916, in the village of Jarnac in western France. After he studied law at the University of Paris, he fought with the French army against Germany in World War II. He then took up government service and politics. He won election as France's first Socialist president in 1981.

Like the Soviets, the French had conducted much financial and military business with Iraq before the Persian Gulf War. They worried that opposing Saddam Hussein might reduce their influence in the Middle East. Even so, the French joined the coalition right after it was formed.

Soon, however, Mitterrand began to express doubts about the use of force against Iraq. He then sent a series of private proposals to Saddam. One proposal would have allowed Iraq to keep part of coastal Kuwait if it withdrew from the rest of the country. Saddam refused to budge. Nor was it likely that the coalition would have agreed to such a generous proposal. That would only have rewarded Saddam for his attack on his neighbor.

Coalition leaders no longer believed that diplomacy could end the conflict, and they grew more and more upset with Mitterrand's independent efforts to make a deal with Saddam.

Despite Mitterrand's actions, on the eve of Desert Storm, he returned France firmly to the coalition fold. He put twenty thousand French troops and two hundred aircraft under coalition command.

French troops performed admirably in the liberation of Kuwait; however, no French companies were asked to take part in the profitable work of rebuilding Kuwait after the war. This reflected the irritation coalition leaders felt when Mitterrand had openly questioned the use of force against Iraq and attempted to negotiate separately with Saddam.

A popular president, Mitterrand remained in office until he retired in 1995. He had served for fourteen years, longer than any other French president. Among his other accomplishments, he is credited in France for his efforts to improve relations with other European nations, Germany in particular. He died in 1996 after a long battle with cancer.

François Mitterrand had doubts about the coalition using force against Iraq. He unsuccessfully tried to talk Saddam into withdrawing from Kuwait.

King Fahd was born in 1923, in Riyadh, the capital of Saudi Arabia. He was the son of King Abdul Aziz (known as Ibn Sa'ud), who founded the Saudi kingdom in 1932. After he received a princely Islamic education and later held several key posts in the Saudi government, Fahd was crowned king in 1982. Fahd also became a leader in the Arab world, and he tried to ease tensions the Middle East.

The new king stayed friendly with the West. This tradition resulted from the help the Saudi monarchy received in its early years. At that time, many experts from the United States and other countries showed the Saudis how to find oil and extract it. Western nations soon became good customers for Saudi oil.

Like so many others in the summer of 1990, the king urged Saddam not to march into Kuwait. When he did, Fahd condemned the invasion and demanded immediate withdrawal. Days later, U.S. secretary of defense Dick Cheney and General Norman Schwarzkopf, commander of U.S. forces in the Persian Gulf, visited the king in his Riyadh palace. The American leaders told the king that Saddam posed a threat to Saudi Arabia. Fahd agreed. He then formally invited U.S. forces to set up bases on its soil. This proved to be a key step in building an international coalition. It also served as an invitation for other Arab states to join the coalition, which many did. The king did not stop there. He also provided the coalition with well-trained Saudi troops.

After the war, Fahd's health

Opposite: When Iraq refused to withdraw from Kuwait, King Fahd asked the United States for military aid to prevent an invasion of Saudi Arabia. Above: Well-trained Saudi soldiers joined coalition forces in Operation Desert Shield.

began to fail. A diabetic, he suffered a stroke in 1995, which forced him to cut back on his official duties. He stopped presiding over Saudi cabinet meetings in 1996. His half-brother, Crown Prince Abdullah, has since taken over many of the king's responsibilities. Selected long ago to succeed Fahd, Abdullah is now widely seen as the acting head of Saudi Arabia.

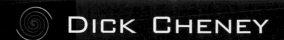
Born on January 30, 1941, in Lincoln, Nebraska, Dick Cheney grew up in Casper, Wyoming. After he earned a master's degree in political science at the University of Wyoming, he moved to Washington, D.C., where he began a career in government. He worked as a special assistant in the Nixon administration, and later as President Gerald Ford's chief of staff. He then won elective office in Wyoming and served five straight terms in Congress. He became the Republican leader in the House of Representatives during his last term. When President George H. W. Bush took office, he selected Cheney to serve as secretary of defense.

Even a month before Saddam's invasion, Cheney had to make sure the U.S. military was prepared to stop any Iraqi advance beyond Kuwait. It also needed to be ready to expel Iraqis from Kuwait, if the president so ordered. The secretary quickly directed his top commanders to send air, ground, and naval forces to the Persian Gulf region. Meanwhile, he met with the defense ministers of other countries. If a multinational coalition were to work, its troops would have to be combined into a single, unified force. It fell mostly to Cheney to arrange such an alliance.

Once it occupied Kuwait, the Iraqi army pushed toward the Kuwait-Saudi border. This aggressive posture prompted Cheney to fly to Saudi Arabia. He brought with him General Norman Schwarzkopf, commander in chief of coalition forces. They warned King Fahd of the threat that faced his country. Convinced, the king agreed to join the newly formed coalition. He also gave it permission to base many of its military operations in Saudi Arabia.

Cheney then embarked on a series of diplomatic missions, all of them designed to enlist as many coalition members as possible. Once he completed that task, he directed the war effort with Schwarzkopf and Joint Chiefs of Staff chairman, General Colin Powell. The secretary also took part in preparations for coalition air patrols over Iraq after the war ended.

When Bush failed to win reelection in 1992, Cheney left government to head a large construction corporation in Wyoming. He returned to the Washington limelight after he was elected vice president of the United States in 2000.

Defense Secretary Dick Cheney helped recruit thirty-five countries to join the coalition. He then directed the war with General Norman Schwarzkopf and General Colin Powell.

Born May 4, 1928, in the Nile delta region of Egypt, Hosni Mubarak chose to follow a military career. He graduated from both the Egyptian Military Academy and the Egyptian Air Force Academy. He climbed steadily in rank and eventually became Egypt's air marshal. In 1975, President Anwar Sadat named him vice president. Six years later, assassins killed Sadat at a military parade. Mubarak took his place.

The new president inherited a troubled relationship with the Arab League. Made up of all the Arab nations, the league had dismissed Egypt as a member after Sadat signed a peace treaty in 1979 with a traditional Arab enemy, Israel. When he became president in 1981, Mubarak urged the league to restore Egypt's membership. It took the league eight years to decide. Not until 1989 did it readmit Egypt to its rolls.

Mubarak regarded the readmission as a personal victory. He had mended relations with the Arab world. Later that year, Kuwait awarded him the "Medal of the Great Mubarak." This prize is named after an important leader in Islamic history, as is the Egyptian president himself.

His reputation in the Arab world on the rise, Mubarak faced an awkward situation when Saddam Hussein threatened Kuwait with invasion. Iraq and Kuwait were both members of the Arab League, and Mubarak was unsure whose side to take. Eventually, he chose a middle ground.

Hosni Mubarak led Egypt into the coalition. Other Arab League members followed his example.

After several attempts to smooth the differences that divided Iraq and Kuwait, Mubarak gave up. Pressed by the United States and the Saudis, he brought Egypt into the coalition. Many members of the Arab League followed his example, to the relief of U.S. leaders—and to the relief of Mubarak, as well.

Egyptians reelected Mubarak president in 1993. He then became an outspoken enemy of his country's Islamic extremists. Such extremists were thought to have made an attempt on his life in 1995. He won reelection to another six-year term in 1999.

Born in Houston, Texas, on April 28, 1930, James Baker attended Princeton University. After he served in the Marine Corps, he attended the University of Texas where he earned a law degree. He first came to Washington in 1975 as undersecretary of commerce under President Gerald Ford. President Ronald Reagan named him secretary of the treasury in 1985, and President George H. W. Bush picked him to serve as secretary of state in 1989.

James Baker (above right and opposite page) voted in the UN Security Council to approve military action against Iraq. Two months later, Congress voted to authorize the use of force against Iraq.

As the nation's top diplomat, Baker soon found himself at an international crossroads in his new job at the State Department. Once Iraq invaded Kuwait, the secretary had to make the American position clear to other countries as well as to the United Nations. In the months following, he also helped enlist various coalition members.

A trip to Moscow in late November 1990 proved crucial to U.S. intentions. At a high-level meeting, Baker won Soviet consent to let the United Nations include three key words in its latest resolution condemning Iraq. The final resolution stated that the coalition could use "all necessary means" to drive Iraq out of Kuwait. These words meant that the UN did not limit the coalition to only economic or political action. Instead, it allowed for the use of military force, if the U.S.–led coalition chose.

The secretary attended another crucial meeting on January 9, 1991, in Geneva, Switzerland. There he met with Tariq Aziz, Iraq's foreign minister. Baker arrived with a letter from Bush to Saddam. It offered him one last chance to withdraw peacefully from Kuwait. After he heard from Baker what the letter contained, Aziz refused to take it to his president. His refusal meant that all hope for a peaceful outcome was lost. Just three days later, the previously hesitant U.S. Congress voted to allow Bush to use force against Iraq. The stage for war was now fully set.

Baker served as secretary of state until August 1992 when he began work as Bush's chief of staff. At the end of the Bush presidency, he moved to Houston to practice law. He remains active in Republican Party politics.

TARIQ AZIZ

SADDAM HUSSEIN'S SPOKESMAN

Born in 1936 near the northern city of Mosul, Tariq Aziz was given the name Michael Yuhanna by his parents. To avoid religious bias against him as a Christian in a mostly Muslim country, he later took his Muslim name. In Arabic, it means "glorious past."

After he earned a degree in English literature at the Baghdad College of Fine Arts, Aziz worked as a journalist. He then became the top editor of the Ba'ath Party's newspaper. From there he moved into government service, where he soon befriended Saddam Hussein. Aziz eventually rose to the combined post of foreign minister and deputy prime minister. In 1980, he survived an assassination attempt.

Even in the months before the invasion of Kuwait, Aziz became as familiar to the world as his notorious leader. As Iraq's chief diplomat, it was his job to explain and justify Saddam's actions to the international community. In one television press conference after another, he lashed out bitterly at other countries. These included Kuwait, Arab members of the coalition, and especially the United States.

Aziz never wavered in reflecting Saddam's hard-line refusal to change his invasion plans, even in Geneva during his memorable meeting with U.S. secretary of state James Baker, when he declined to

Opposite: Tariq Aziz refused to deliver a letter from Bush to Saddam demanding Iraq's withdrawal from Kuwait. Above: Aziz tried unsuccessfully to convince Egypt's Hosni Mubarak to support Iraq's invasion of Kuwait.

deliver to Saddam a last-chance letter from U.S. president George H.W. Bush. The letter demanded that Iraqis withdraw from Kuwait.

Aziz remained dutifully loyal to Saddam once the coalition scored its quick and decisive victory. He vigorously defended his government's brutal assault on the country's rebellious Shiites and Kurds, which took place soon after the war ended. Aziz also resumed his role as Saddam's main spokesman.

In early 2003, a new coalition, again led by U.S. and British forces, invaded Iraq after Saddam Hussein repeatedly refused to cooperate with UN weapons inspectors. Baghdad fell to coalition forces in April, and two weeks later, Aziz was taken into U.S. custody. His long service as Saddam's spokesman was at an end.

COLIN L. POWELL

Born in New York's Harlem on April 5, 1937, Colin L. Powell was raised in the South Bronx by Jamaican American parents. He earned a bachelor's degree at the City College of New York in 1958, and then joined the U.S. Army as a second lieutenant. After he reached the rank of four-star general, he was named chairman of the Joint Chiefs of Staff, the highest position in the American military. The chairman acts as the main link between the armed forces and the president and his secretary of defense.

Experienced in combat, Powell knew the high cost of war in lives and money. As chairman, he wanted political leaders to give the military a clear mission before entering any war. Once they did, they would need to provide enough resources so the military could win an overwhelming victory in a very short period of time.

Colin Powell (above and opposite) used his years of U.S. Army experience in directing the military strategy of Operations Desert Shield and Desert Storm.

President George H. W. Bush and Secretary of Defense Dick Cheney agreed. Once the president decided to defend the Saudis, Powell ordered some 250,000 U.S. troops, hundreds of ships, and thousands of planes and tanks to the desert kingdom. This signaled the start of Operation Desert Shield. When the president later decided to liberate Kuwait, Powell sent an additional 200,000 troops. Coalition forces were then strong enough to launch Operation Desert Storm. Under the direction of Bush, Cheney, and Powell, General Norman Schwarzkopf carried out the military strategy that led to a swirl victory in Kuwait.

Powell retired from the military in September 1993. He then wrote his autobiography and became a popular public speaker. He also refused to start a political career despite pressure to do so by both Republicans and Democrats. In December 2000, President George W. Bush nominated him as secretary of state. He was sworn into that office on January 20, 2001.

H. NORMAN SCHWARZKOPF

DESIGNED THE BATTLE PLAN FOR DESERT STORM

The son of an army general, H. Norman Schwarzkopf was born on August 22, 1934, in Trenton, New Jersey. A graduate of the U. S. Military Academy at West Point, New York, his career included combat action in Vietnam and Grenada, desk jobs at the Pentagon, and command positions with several infantry divisions. Over the years, his sharp mind and quick temper earned him the nickname "Stormin' Norman."

By then a four-star general, Schwarzkopf was named commander of the U.S. Army Central Command in 1988. Soon after his appointment, the general ordered his staff to conduct a computerized war game. Designed to show how Persian Gulf oil fields could be defended, it included a careful evaluation of Iraqi forces. A few months later, Iraq invaded Kuwait, but Schwarzkopf had done his homework. The instructive war game had fully prepared him to block further Iraqi advances.

Schwarzkopf's greatest achievements lay in the plan he drew up for Desert Storm and in the skillful execution of that plan. The operation called for air attacks to weaken Iraqi reinforcements clustered just outside Kuwait, followed by a ground war launched from Saudi Arabia.

Schwarzkopf's ground-war plan involved tricking the Iraqis into believing that the coalition would attack from the waters of the Persian Gulf. U.S. Marines and other units instead mounted a real attack from the Saudi border directly into Kuwait City. Also according to Schwarzkopf's plan, another powerful coalition force swept undetected around Kuwait's western and northern border with Iraq. This sweep flattened the Iraqis.

General Norman Schwarzkopf (above, second from left) planned and executed Operation Desert Storm so skillfully that it was one of the shortest and most successful wars in military history.

Iraq surrendered less than one hundred hours after the ground war began. Schwarzkopf had led one of the most successful—and shortest—wars in military history.

Schwarzkopf retired from active duty a few months after the conclusion of the war. He has since written his autobiography and become a featured speaker who attracts large audiences across the country. When the 1999 presidential election approached, Schwarzkopf made many speeches in support of candidate George W. Bush.

Born in a rural Syrian village on October 6, 1930, Hafiz al-Assad became a fighter pilot and received combat flight training in the Soviet Union and Egypt. He rose in rank to become commander of the Syrian air force before he took over as secretary of defense. By then he had become a leading figure in Syria's Ba'ath Party. He was elected president in 1971 and was reelected for three seven-year terms after that.

Opposite: Syrian president Hafiz al-Assad realized he would need financial help from the West after the breakup of the Soviet Union. Above: Syria joined the coalition and sent military forces to fight Iraq.

Assad controlled his country with the same strong-arm tactics Saddam Hussein used in Iraq. Although both countries are neighboring Arab states, their two leaders disliked each other intensely. Each saw the other as a rival in the often heated mix of Middle East politics. The same dislike and rivalry existed between the Iraqi branch of the Ba'ath Party and the Syrian branch. It came as no surprise when Syria supported Iran in its war with Iraq.

During the 1970s and 1980s, the Soviet Union gave Syria billions of dollars to build up its armed forces. When it seemed apparent that the Soviet Union would break up, Assad needed to find another source for financial aid. He looked shrewdly toward the Western nations. Iraq's invasion of Kuwait gave him the perfect chance to carry favor with this possible new source. Along with several other Arab countries, Syria joined the coalition and contributed substantial military forces to fight Saddam.

The United States was particularly grateful for this show of support. Soon after the war ended, the United States and Kuwait rewarded Syria with billions of dollars in aid. Nonetheless, Assad came to openly resent the heightened influence of the United States in the Middle East.

When his health began to fail in the mid-1990s, Assad set out to pave the way for his son Bashar to succeed him. He accomplished his aim by ruthless means. He either fired or sent into exile anyone in government who might challenge Bashar for the presidency. When Assad died on June 10, 2000, his son became Syria's president.

YITZHAK SHAMIR

Born in eastern Poland in 1915, Shamir left Warsaw University at age twenty to go to British-controlled Palestine. He resumed his law studies in Jerusalem. At the same time he founded an underground group violently opposed to British rule. After two arrests and two escapes from British prisons, he was granted asylum in France. He returned to Jerusalem in 1948, just before Israel became an independent state. Two years later, Shamir joined the Mossad, Israel's intelligence agency. He entered politics in 1970 and became foreign minister in 1983 and prime minister in 1984.

Above: Iraq fired Scud missiles into Tel Aviv in an attempt to draw Israel into the war, but Israel did not order a military response. Opposite: Yitzhak Shamir was later praised by the coalition for his restraint.

A man of action, Shamir, prime minister during the Gulf War, restrained himself at the right time. In an attempt to draw Israel into the war, Iraq fired Russian-built Scud missiles into Israel. As the missiles rained down, Shamir did not order a military response. Coalition leaders had asked him not to. They feared that any such action would drive Arab partners out of the coalition because such partners were unlikely to fight at the side of Israel, their long-time enemy.

Therefore, Shamir had little choice but to avoid striking back. All he could do was provide every Israeli citizen with a gas mask because the Scuds might be carrying chemical warheads.

They were not. Nor did the missiles do much damage. After the war, Shamir was widely praised for his restraint. The coalition's crucial Arab members had not left, and the coalition had stuck together.

Shamir remained prime minister until 1992 when his party, the Likud, lost the general election. He then stepped down as the party's leader. He retired from politics in 1996.

JABIR AL-AHMAD AL SABAH

KUWAITI EMIR FORMED A GOVERNMENT IN EXILE

Born to the royal Al Sabah family sometime in 1929, Jabir al-Ahmad Al Sabah was homeschooled, largely by palace tutors in Kuwait City. Because members of the royal family hold most high positions in Kuwait's oil industry, as well as in its government, he became head of security at a group of oilfields at age twenty. Sabah later became minister of finance and industry, and then prime minister. In 1977 he succeeded his cousin and became emir of Kuwait.

On the day Iraq invaded his country, Sabah and several other members of the royal family fled to Saudi Arabia. By some Saudi accounts, they lived in their temporary quarters in the same luxury they had long enjoyed in Kuwait City. Their lavish ways had long irked many Saudis, as well as many other Arabs in the Middle East, Saddam Hussein among them. While the Iraqi leader was no stranger to luxury himself, he still resented Sabah for his oil policies and for his friendship with the United States and other Western countries.

Sabah did not stay idle after finding a comfortable haven. Once settled in, he formed a government in exile. He also began to beam radio broadcasts to his subjects in besieged Kuwait.

His messages urged them to stiffly resist the invaders. Some obeyed and defied the enemy. This made the Iraqi occupation more difficult than expected. Most Kuwaitis, however, did not have the weapons or the will to fight back. Innocent victims, thousands of them were killed, wounded, or jailed by rampaging Iraqi troops.

Above: Kuwaitis showed their support for Emir Sabah after the liberation of Kuwait. Right: After seven months in exile, Sabah returned to govern his country.

While still in exile, Sabah reached a settlement with his political opponents back home. He agreed to restore Kuwait's national assembly, which he had earlier dissolved when it questioned the government's competence.

Sabah and his entourage did not return to Kuwait until more than a month after the war officially ended in April 1991. His looted and damaged palace became one of the first structures to be rebuilt in his war-torn country. In 1992, the emir made good on his promise to restore the national assembly.

⊚ CHRONOLOGY

August 1988	Iran-Iraq War ends.
July 17, 1990	Saddam publicly threatens war with Kuwait.
July 21, 1990	Iraqi forces move toward Kuwait border.
August 2, 1990	Iraq invades. United Nations calls for Iraq to withdraw.
August 3, 1990	Bush and Thatcher meet in Colorado.
August 5, 1990	Bush declares invasion "will not stand."
August 6, 1990	Cheney and Schwarzkopf convince King Fahd that Iraq is ready to invade his country. He requests U.S. military aid.
August 8, 1990	First U.S. fighter planes land in Saudi Arabia. Britain commits air and naval forces for Saudi defense.
August 28, 1990	Iraq claims Kuwait as its nineteenth province.
November 29, 1990	UN Security Council authorizes use of "all means necessary" to eject Iraq from Kuwait.
January 9, 1991	Baker meets Tariq Aziz in Geneva in last try for peaceful solution.
January 15, 1991	UN deadline for Iraqi withdrawal not met.
January 17, 1991	Desert Storm launched as coalition air war begins.
January 18, 1991	First Scuds hit Israel.
January 22, 1991	Iraq fires ten Scuds into Saudi Arabia.
January 23, 1991	Iraqis start torching Kuwaiti oil wells and dumping oil into the gulf.
February 11, 1991	Air war intensifies. Guided missiles and bombs continue to hit Iraqi military targets.
February 24, 1991	Ground war begins.
February 26, 1991	Iraqis flee Kuwait City.
February 28, 1991	Ground war ends after only one hundred hours. Cease-fire takes effect.
April 11, 1991	Gulf War officially ends after Iraq accepts UN cease-fire resolution.

For Further Information

Books

Kathlyn Gay, *Persian Gulf War*. New York: Millbrook, 2003.

Karen Price Hossell, *The Persian Gulf War*. Portsmouth, NH: Heinemann Library, 2003.

Zachary Kent, *The Mother of All Battles*. Berkeley Heights, NJ: Enslow, 1994.

Angelia L. Mance, *Iraq*. Broomall, PA: Chelsea House, 2003.

Peggy J. Parks, *Nations in Conflict: Iraq*. San Diego: Blackbirch, 2003.

Websites

The Gulf War: An Oral History
www.pbs.org
This site features a PBS Frontline oral history of the Persian Gulf War.

The Unfinished War
www.cnn.com
CNN's lively retrospective of the first televised war.

Themepark: Liberty
www.uen.org
This Utah Education Network site contains many useful links to information about the Persian Gulf War.

Flashback: Desert Storm http://news.bbc.co.uk
A flashback of Persian Gulf War from a British viewpoint.

About The Author

Donna Schaffer is a writer and editor who lives in New York State.